The Trouble with Mum

EGMONT

For Asha, Maya and Torah –
whose Mums are no trouble at all!

The Trouble with Mum

Babette Cole

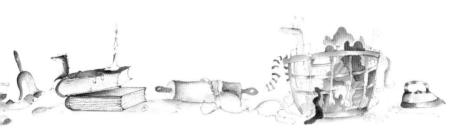

The trouble with
mum is the hats
she wears . . .

At first, other kids gave me funny looks when,

she took me to my new school . . .

She didn't seem to get on . . .

with the other parents.

They kept asking me where my dad was.
Mum says he's staying put
until he stops going to the pub!

Teacher asked us if our mums would
make cakes for the school governors'
tea . . .

Mum made some.

They were a disaster,
but the kids thought they were
BRILLIANT!

They asked if they could come and play at my house.

I didn't know
what they would
think of it!

Their parents said
they couldn't come,
but they came
anyway.

They liked our pets.

They met Gran.

Mum behaved very well.

We all went wild!

Then their parents turned up
and ruined everything.

They told Mum off.

Mum
was
sad.

My new friends were fed up.
They said, "Your mum's O.K. But we're
not allowed to come and play any more."

Then one day the school caught fire.
We thought we were going to roast.

Mum beat all the fire engines!

She put out the fire
before any of
the parents
arrived.

They couldn't thank her enough.

Now we all go wild
at my house.

First published in Great Britain by Kaye and Ward Ltd in 1983
This edition published in 2004
Reprinted in 1986 by Egmont Books Limited,
239 Kensington High Street,
London W8 6SA

Text and illustrations copyright © Babette Cole 1983
Babette Cole has asserted her moral rights.
3 5 7 9 10 8 6 4
1 4052 1121 0
Printed and Bound in China

A CIP catalogue record for this title
is available from the British Library.